A Tale of
TWO Goats

Tom Barber

illustrated by Rosalind Beardshaw

To all of my mothers and fathers,
without whom I wouldn't have been possible
T.B.

For Kate, Paul and Loki
R. B. x

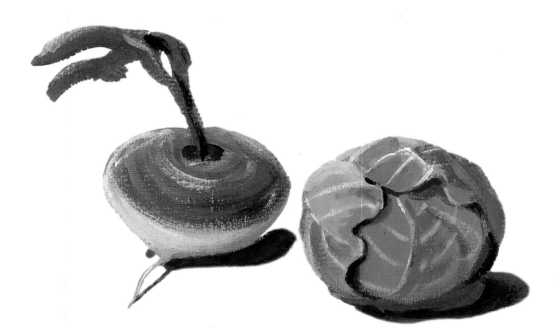

First edition for the United States, its territories and dependencies and Canada published in
2005 by Barron's Educational Series, Inc.

First published in Great Britain in 2005 by Gullane Children's Books,
an imprint of Pinwheel Limited, 259-269 Old Marylebone Road, London, NW1 5XJ

Text © Tom Barber 2005
Illustrations © Rosalind Beardshaw 2005

All inquiries should be addressed to:
Barron's Educational Series, Inc.
250 Wireless Blvd.
Hauppauge, NY 11788
www.barronseduc.com

International Standard Book No.: 0-7641-5847-3

Library of Congress Catalog No.: 2004112281

Printed and bound in China
9 8 7 6 5 4 3 2 1

A Tale of
TWO Goats

Tom Barber

illustrated by Rosalind Beardshaw

Farmer Cole lived all alone on a big farm in the middle of the prairie. His only companion was a goat named Myrtle. Every morning after milking he set her loose in a field of cabbages.

Next door was another big farm. Here lived Farmer Jones,
all on his own as well. His only friend was a goat named Muriel.
Every morning after milking he set her loose in a field of turnips.

Between Myrtle's field of cabbages and Muriel's field of turnips ran a fence of wood and wire. It had been started by Farmer Cole and added to by Farmer Jones. "It's the only way to stop his greedy goat from making off with my vegetables," both farmers said to themselves.

Things may have stayed like this forever,
had it not been for one surprising fact. Myrtle,
with her cabbages, preferred turnips, and
Muriel, with her turnips, preferred cabbages.

Now, you must know
that nothing can come between a goat
and its stomach. So Myrtle and Muriel had come
up with a perfect solution to their problem. Every day,
Myrtle pushed a piece of cabbage through the wire to Muriel.
Muriel, in turn, pushed a piece of turnip through to Myrtle. This kept
them both happy, and over the years they became close friends.

But then came the fateful day when Farmer Cole and
Farmer Jones finally noticed what the goats were up to.
"I can't have his goat eating my cabbages,"
said Farmer Cole.
"I can't have his goat tasting my turnips,"
said Farmer Jones.
"This must stop!" they both said.

So Farmer Cole
and Farmer
Jones gathered
some wood
and nails.

Then they
began
hammering
and
sawing,
each acting
as if the other
one simply
wasn't there.

They only stopped when there was not the tiniest
gap left where the goats might push through a morsel.

But goats' teeth are miraculously strong, and
the very next day Myrtle and Muriel gnawed a hole
right through the fence and carried on exactly as before.
Farmer Cole and Farmer Jones were on the lookout for
trouble now. "This won't do at all," they muttered to themselves.

They brought bricks and
mortar and, in place of the fence,
they built a wall. Even a goat
can't chew through bricks!

But goats can dig when they put their minds to it.
So the very next day, Myrtle and Muriel tunneled
right underneath the wall. They met up in the middle
and swapped turnip for cabbage as usual.

Well, the farmers weren't going to put up with that! They each dug a trench along their side of the wall and filled it in with concrete. *This will put a stop to that nonsense,* they thought.

And it did – for a while! But goats can throw
pretty well. So Myrtle and Muriel tossed the turnips
and cabbages over the wall to each other.

That took care of the food. But the truth was the two goats were missing the old days, when they could chat with each other, face to face, through the fence.

Meanwhile, Farmer Cole and Farmer Jones built the wall higher.

But goats, as you know,
are expert climbers!

So Farmer Cole and
Farmer Jones built the
wall even higher!

But goats can do a mean polevault—
really, I've seen them!

Farmer Cole and Farmer Jones had no choice but to build
the wall even higher. They topped it off with coils of wire.
"That should finish off their little game," they
said to themselves. And, indeed, it did.

But now there was a new problem. Myrtle stopped eating her food. All she could do was stare at the wall and bleat sadly. From the other side came a faint answering bleat, for things were just as bad with Muriel.

Farmer Cole and Farmer Jones
were worried. They tried
everything – pea soup . . .

. . . peeled carrots,
straw hats . . .

. . . even a turnip and a
cabbage! But neither
Myrtle or Muriel would
take even a bite.

Soon Myrtle and Muriel were nothing more than bags of bones. Farmer Cole and Farmer Jones were at their wits' end. As a last resort, they called in the veterinarian, who told them both the same thing. It was a restless night for the farmers and, in the morning, they both carried their goats down to the field. Then they went back to fetch their tractors.

In ten minutes flat, the wall was smashed to the ground! Farmer Cole and Farmer Jones gazed at each other over the rubble. For the first time ever, instead of looking away, they gave each other a shy wave.

With the wall down, Myrtle and
Muriel struggled to their feet.
It was a touching reunion.

Myrtle was soon shredding a cabbage while Muriel was on her second turnip. Farmer Cole and Farmer Jones were so relieved to see their goats happy again. And with the fence gone, it was hard to ignore each other. Soon they were chatting away. It was amazing what they found to talk about – tractors, vegetables, milk – and goats!

Farmer Cole and Farmer Jones still
live on their own, but they have their goats
and they have each other, and that seems
enough for all four of them.